by Verity Craig

First edition.

The author Verity Craig will not be held responsible for any third parties, businesses or websites referred to in this book.

Although the author has made every effort to ensure that the information in this book was correct at press time, the author and publisher do not assume and hereby disclaim any liability to any party for any loss, damage, or disruption caused by errors or omissions, whether such errors or omissions result from negligence, accident, or any other cause.

ISBN **978-1-3999-3746-7**

Written by Verity Craig
Illustrated by Imashi Opatha (comic.factory.productions@gmail.com)
Published by Chocolate Box Publishing

Printed & Published in United Kingdom

Dedicated
to
my
GIRLS

CHAPTER 01
Meeting Friends

Once upon a time, there was a little bear called **Baggy Pants.**

He was called **'Baggy Pants'** because his trousers were too big for him and so sometimes they would fall down.

He didn't mind being called **Baggy Pants;** his family and friends called him by that name,

and he loved them

. . . and more importantly they loved him.

It was a sunny spring day in Brissel Bush Woods where Baggy Pants and his family lived.

And on such sunny days, he would walk to school.

On this particular morning, Baggy Pants grabbed his school bag and his mummy handed him his packed lunch.

"There you are Baggy Pants" she said
"You have your favourite today . . .
jam and ham pizza!"

"Yum," said Baggy Pants,
"Thank you Mummy!"
It was a peculiar combination, but one the little bear loved.

Off Baggy Pants set, down Pocket Lane towards his school.

On the way, he passed his friend Benjamin's house.

"Hello Benji,"

he called out to his Panda bear friend who he spotted playing in his front garden.

"Are you walking to school with me today?"
Benjamin looked up and saw Baggy Pants.

"No, Baggy Pants. I've had a sore throat so my Mummy thinks it best I stay home today. Sorry."

Baggy Pants Bear looked sad,
"Oh dear. Well, I hope you feel better soon Benji. Bye."

And he continued his walk to school.

Soon he was by his friend Sally's house. She was a white polar bear teddy. He could see her sitting on her doorstep.

"Good morning Sally. Are you walking to school with me today?"

Sally looked sad as she looked up,

"No, I am not going to school today Baggy Pants.
when I was playing on the swing
yesterday after school,
I fell off and hurt my ankle.
Mummy and Daddy said
it's best I stay home
today to let it rest."

Baggy Pants felt sad,

"Oh, ok," said the little bear to Sally.
"Well, I hope your ankle gets better soon! Bye."
And he continued his walk to school.

Just then, he saw his friend Peter, a long haired little grizzly bear, sitting on the wall outside of his front garden whistling to himself.

"Good morning Peter," Baggy Pants called to his friend, "I'm on my way to school. Are you coming with me?"

Peter looked sad and held up his right paw which had a bandage on it.

"Hello Baggy Pants. I wish I was. But I've got a sore finger from touching a hot pan when my mummy was cooking our dinner last night. So Mummy wants me to stay home today. Sorry."

"Oh dear . . ." said Baggy Pants looking very sad indeed now.

"Well, I hope your finger gets better soon Peter. And don't touch hot pans again."

And off Baggy Pants continued with his walk . . .

alone!

A
6
SCIENCE
SOCIAL STUDIES
MATHS
2x2=4
3x3=9
4x4=16

CHAPTER 02

Begining Of The Peculiar Day

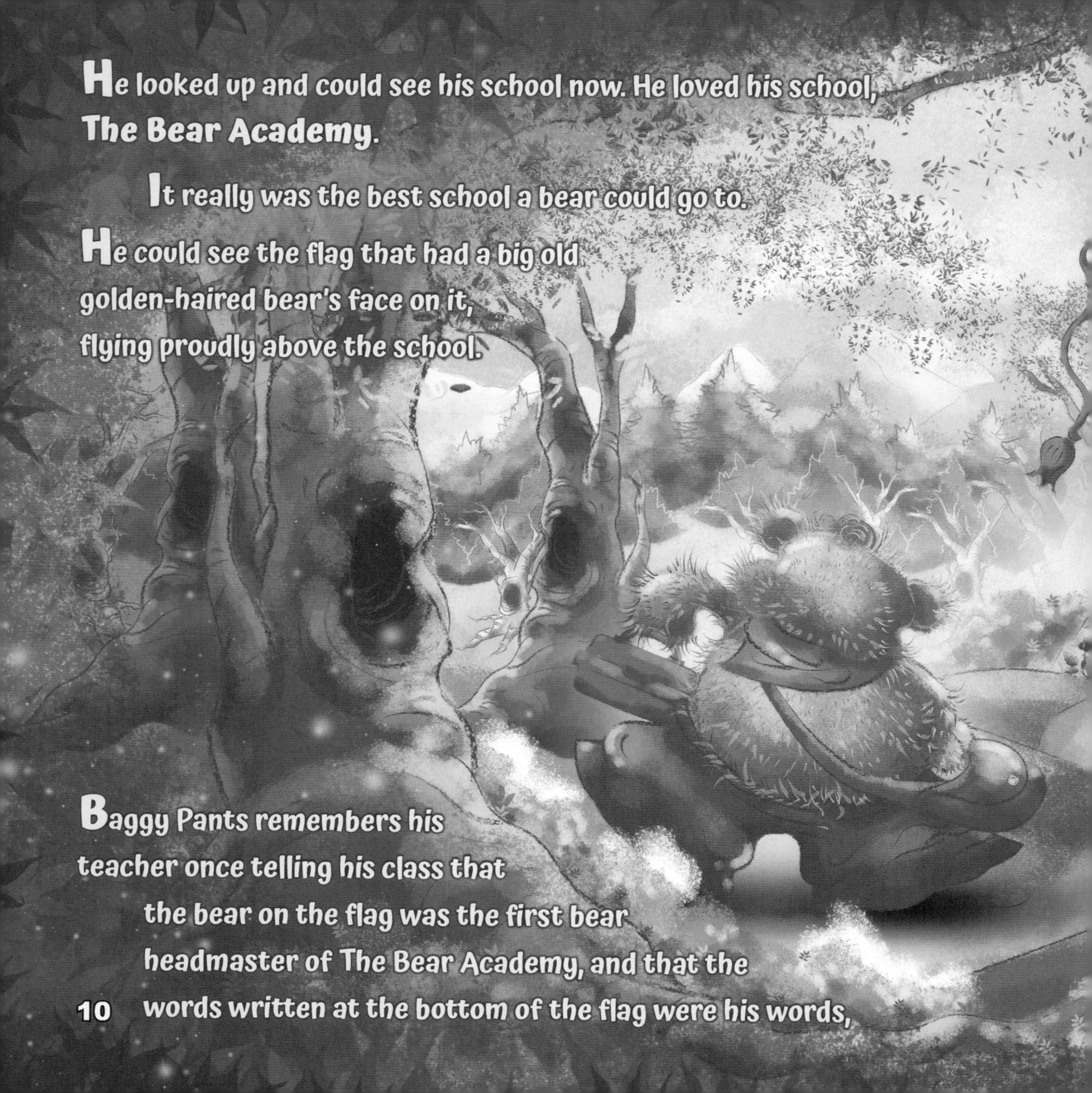

He looked up and could see his school now. He loved his school, The Bear Academy.

It really was the best school a bear could go to.

He could see the flag that had a big old golden-haired bear's face on it, flying proudly above the school.

Baggy Pants remembers his teacher once telling his class that the bear on the flag was the first bear headmaster of The Bear Academy, and that the words written at the bottom of the flag were his words,

"Bears be kind, bears be courageous,
bears have fun!"

As he stepped inside his school, he found his named peg, placed his school bag on it and put his packed lunch on the lunch shelf opposite.

Then, he entered his classroom.

He went and sat down at his desk.

Then he stopped still and looked around.

Something was different. Very different. It was quiet too.

And then Baggy Pants realised . . .

He was the only one there!

Where was everyone?

Suddenly the classroom door flung open with a Whoosh ! ! !
It was Mr Button,
his teacher.

He was a gigantic bear with huge brown eyes
and a big round nose (and heavy loud feet!)
And his paws were the biggest Baggy Pants
had ever seen.

And because he was so big and loud,
Baggy Pants was a little bit scared of him. !

Mr Button placed his files on his big desk with a loud thump and then looked up,

"Good morning bears . . ."

He bellowed in his loud voice.

Then he stopped as he looked at the little bear sitting all on his own in the classroom.

"Baggy Pants . . . where is everyone?"

He shouted as if Baggy Pants should know.

Baggy Pants felt nervous,
as if it was his fault that no one was there.

"Well, Mr Button,"
he started,

"Benjamin has a sore throat,
Sally has a bad ankle
and Peter has a sore finger . . . !"

"I'm not sure about the rest though Mr Button."

"Well, well, well . . .!"

Said the big bear in his loud booming voice tapping his large paws on his desk.

"Looks like it's just you and me today then Baggy Pants!"

"Ye . . . ye . . . yes Sir,"

said Baggy Pants rather nervously.

"Right, well follow me then bear!" said Mr Button.

And off the two bears went.

Baggy Pants followed his tall teacher down the long corridor past the older bears' classrooms,

round the corner past the bear library,

through the door out across the playground and carried on along the path towards the big playing field.

All Baggy Pants kept thinking was,

"Where are we going?"

"He felt like a soldier following his sergeant!"

CHAPTER 03

Tiring . . . But Amazing !

As they passed the glass windows at the side of the indoor swimming pool, Mr Button stopped suddenly.

"Right. Here we are!"

He said with authority,
as he opened
the swimming pool door.

"This pool area has needed a good clean for a long time.
So today, you and I are going to sweep,
mop and scrub in here . . .

and if you do a good job
Baggy Pants,
we may go for a quick dip!".
Continued Mr. Button.

"Does that sound good to you?"

And with that, Baggy Pants had a huge beaming smile on his face and started jumping up and down,

"Yes please sir, that would be amazing . . . !"

Baggy Pants loved swimming.

But as he jumped up and down excitedly, like his namesake, his trousers started falling down to his ankles.

"Baggy Pants, pull up your baggy trousers . . . and lets get cleaning!"

Boomed Mr Button as he clapped his hands together.

So, the two bears set about sweeping, scrubbing and mopping the floors all around the swimming pool.

It was tiring work, and took a long time to do,

but Baggy Pants actually enjoyed it . . . !

The pool area was now gleaming. . . !

They had never seen it so clean.

Soon the two bears were finished...and quite exhausted.

"Right Baggy Pants,"

said Mr Button in his usual loud voice,

"Go and get a pair of the spare swimming trunks on and lets have a jolly old splash!"

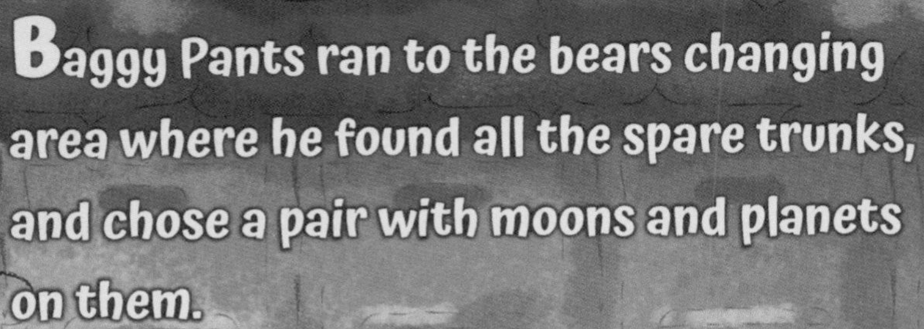

Baggy Pants ran to the bears changing area where he found all the spare trunks, and chose a pair with moons and planets on them.

Excitedly, he hurried on out to the swimming pool in them. . . . ,

As he looked at the water, he had the shock of his life . . . !

Big, tall, old, strict Mr Button was floating around on a pink blow up rubber ring splashing around like a child.

"Come on in
Baggy Pants!"

he called . . .
in what sounded now like a
slightly softer and more fun voice.

"We deserve a little fun after
all that hard work,

don't you think?"

Baggy Pants had the biggest smile on his face ever.

"Wait till I tell all my friends about this,"

he thought.

And he took a big leap and
a jump in to the pool. . . . !

Splash . . . !

He splashed around all afternoon
with Mr Button, right until the bell rang
and school was finished!

CHAPTER 04

A Brilliant Day !

When Baggy Pants returned home, his mummy was setting the table for his supper. . . .

"Hello my little bear,
how was school today?"

She said when she saw him.

"Hello Mummy . . ."

Said Baggy Pants,

"Well, poor Benji had a sore throat
so he wasn't at school,
nor was Sally because
she hurt her ankle,

. . . or
Peter, because he had a sore finger . . .
and no one else in my class arrived either."

His mummy looked surprised and sad for Baggy Pants,

"Oh gosh . . . !" she gasped,

"So you were the only one there?

My poor little bear . . ."

And she patted him gently on his head.

"No, Mummy . . it was a brilliant day in the end," explained Baggy Pants.
"Mr. Button and I cleaned the swimming pool area . . ."

"Oh dear,"
said his mummy frowning,
concerned that he wouldn't have enjoyed that.

Baggy Pants continued,
"And we made everything
gleaming and shiny Mummy.
And then, Mr Button and
I went swimming and we
had the whole swimming
pool to ourselves!
And he's great fun
actually
Mummy . . . !"

Baggy Pants

His mummy laughed,

"My, my, my . . . what a fun day you've had then.

And I thought you weren't so sure about Mr Button with 'the loudest voice' you said you've ever heard . . . ?"

"Mummy, he's the best teacher . . . EVER!"

exclaimed Baggy Pants
to his mummy with a jump,

to which his
trousers once again
needed pulling up!

And with that, the little bear sat down to enjoy his dinner and kept thinking about all the fun he and his teacher had enjoyed together ...!

He hoped tomorrow
would be
just as fun!